PRESENTED TO

....

FROM

....

DATE

....

Because I Love You

ILLUSTRATIONS BY MITCHELL HEINZE

Max Lucado

CROSSWAY BOOKS · WHEATON, ILLINOIS

A DIVISION OF GOOD NEWS PUBLISHERS

PUBLISHER'S ACKNOWLEDGMENT

The publisher wishes to acknowledge that the text for *Because I Love You*
appeared originally as "The Fall" in *Tell Me the Story* © 1992, written by Max
Lucado and illustrated by Ron DiCianni. Special thanks to Ron DiCianni for
the idea and vision behind the creation of the series. For more stories in the "Tell
Me" series, *Tell Me the Story, Tell Me the Secrets, Tell Me the Promises,* and *Tell Me
the Truth,* all published by Crossway Books, are available at your local bookstore.

Because I Love You

Text copyright ©1999 by Max Lucado

Illustrations copyright ©1999 by Mitchell Heinze

Published by Crossway Books

a division of Good News Publishers

1300 Crescent Street

Wheaton, Illinois 60187

Illustrations by Mitchell Heinze

Design by Big Picture Design / D^2 DesignWorks

First printing 1999

Printed in the United States of America

LIBRARY OF CONGRESS CATALOGING-IN-PUBLICATION DATA

Lucado, Max.
    Because I love you/Max Lucado: illustrated by Mitch Heinze.
      p. cm.
      Summary: Shaddai, a wise and loving man, builds a wonderful village for his children, but
when one of them chooses to go out into the dangerous wilderness, Shaddai does not abandon him.
     ISBN 0-89107-992-0 (alk.paper)
     [1. Christian life—Fiction. 2. Allegories.] I. Heinze, Mitchell, ill. II. Title.
PZ7.L9684Be 1999
[Fic]—dc21
                                    97-48306
                                    CIP
                                    AC

08   07   06   05   04   03   02   01   00   99

15 14 13 12 11 10 9 8 7 6 5 4 3

TO ALL HANDICAPPED CHILDREN

God Loves You!

ong ago in a land far away and unlike any you've ever seen, there lived a wise man named Shaddai. Shaddai was a large man with a tender heart. He had bright blue eyes and a long, thick beard. When he laughed, which is something he did often, his cheeks would lift until his eyes became half-moons of joy.

When he sang, which is something else he did often, everything stopped to listen. Tall aspens would bend. Squirrels, butterflies, and birds would pause. Even the children would turn when they heard his voice. And well they should. It was for them he sang.

And for the children, Shaddai had built a wonderful village. It was more than any child could dream. The children plunged into the sky-blue pond. They squealed as they soared high on the swings hung from the apple tree branches. They scampered through the meadows and giggled in the orchards. The sun never seemed to set too early, and the cool night sky always brought a quiet peace. And, most of all, Shaddai was always near.

When Shaddai wasn't in the meadow with the children or in the orchards with the children, he was in the workshop—with the children. They loved to be with him while he worked. They loved to smell the sawdust, hear him sing, and watch him carve a chair out of a log or make a table out of a tree. They would gather around him and take turns pressing their tiny hands flat against his great big one.

Every night he would gather the children on the grassy meadow and tell them stories. Fascinated, the children would listen as long as Shaddai—or their weary eyes—allowed.

The children loved Shaddai. And Shaddai loved the children. He knew each one by name, and he knew everything about them. He knew Lucy's love of birds. He knew Roland's fear of darkness. He knew Daphne was friendly and Spencer was shy. He knew Paladin was curious. When one of them called his name, he dropped whatever he was doing and turned. His giant heart had a hundred strings—each held by a different child. And Shaddai loved each one the same.

That's why he built the wall.

The wall was a high stone fence surrounding the village. Shaddai had built it, rock upon rock. The wall was so tall it stood high above Shaddai. Even if he stretched his arms as high as he could, he still couldn't touch the top of the wall. He spent days building it. And as he built, he did not sing.

A deadly forest stood outside the village. As Shaddai built the fence, he would often pause and look into the shadows beyond. Cruel thorns and savage beasts and hidden pits filled the dark forest. It was no place for the children Shaddai loved.

"Beyond the wall is danger," he would tell the children in solemn tones. "You were made for my village, not for the terrible land beyond. Stay with me. It's safe here."

But in his heart he knew it was only a matter of time.

The day he placed the final stone on the wall, he returned to his shop, took a long aspen branch, sat down at his bench, and carved a staff. Shaddai stood the staff in a corner. "I'll be ready," he told himself.

Sometime later a boy ran into Shaddai's workshop. The sandy-haired child with searching eyes and restless energy brought the Maker both joy and concern.

"Shaddai!"

In one motion the Maker dropped his hammer and turned. "What is it, Paladin?"

The boy spoke in spurts as he gasped for air. "The wall…I found a… hole. It's a big opening, sir." The boy's hands stretched to show the size. "Someone could crawl through it."

Shaddai pulled over a stool and sat down. "I knew it would be you, Paladin, my child. Tell me, how did you find it?"

"I was walking along the wall searching for—"

"Holes?"

Paladin paused, surprised that Shaddai knew. "Yes, I was looking for holes."

"So you could see out into the forest?"

"I was curious, Shaddai. I wanted to know why you won't let us go out there. Why is it so bad?"

Shaddai motioned for the boy to come to him. When Paladin came near, the Maker cupped the small face in his hands and lifted it so the boy would look directly into his eyes. The urgency of the look caused Paladin's stomach to feel empty.

"Paladin, listen to me. The lands out there are not for you. They are not for me. A journey into the forest will hurt you. You were not made for those lands. Let your feet carry you to the many places you can go—not to the one place you can't. If you leave here, you will not find the way back."

Paladin spoke softly. "You will fix the hole then?"

"No, Paladin, I created the hole because I love you so much."

"But you just said you don't want us to leave."

"I don't want you to leave. I want you to stay with me, but I did make the opening when I built the wall."

"But if you don't fix it," said Paladin, "the children might leave."

"I know, Paladin. But I want the children to stay because they *want* to, not because they *have* to."

Paladin didn't understand. Uncomfortable, he turned to leave. He needed to think about what Shaddai had said. As he entered the sunlight, he looked back into the shop. There sat Shaddai, leaning backward, still watching.

Paladin was confused. Part of him wanted the safety of Shaddai's shop, while another part drew him toward the fence. He looked again into the shop. Shaddai was standing now—not moving, but standing. His large hand stretched out to the boy.

Paladin turned quickly away, as if he hadn't seen. He walked as fast as he could, aimlessly at first, then purposely toward the fence.

"I won't get too near," he said to himself. "I'll just peek out."

Questions came as quickly as his steps. *Why do I want to do what Shaddai doesn't want me to do? Why am I so curious? Is it so wrong to want to see beyond the fence?*

By now Paladin was at the hole. Without stopping to think, he lay on his stomach and squirmed through just far enough to stick his head out the other side.

"I'll just take a quick look," he told himself. "What could be wrong with that? Shaddai said he made the hole because he loved us. I wonder what he's keeping from me?"

As if his knees were moving on their own, Paladin crawled farther. Soon he was through the hole and on the outside of the wall. He rose slowly to his feet. For several moments he didn't move. He wondered if something would come out of the trees to hurt him. Nothing did. He relaxed his shoulders and sighed. "Hmmm… It's not so bad," he said aloud. "It's nice out here. What was Shaddai worried about?"

Paladin began walking into the forest. Twigs snapped beneath his bare feet. Sweet flowers scented the air. *I don't see any scary creatures*, he thought. The trees were so thick he could barely see the sky. "Just a few steps into the woods," he said aloud, "to see what it's like."

After a dozen more steps, he stopped. He liked the wilderness. "Nothing to fear here." For the first time in his young life, he believed that Shaddai was wrong. "Just wait until I tell the others." And he turned to go back through the hole.

But the hole was gone!

He stopped and stared. He saw only a solid wall. Paladin ran to the wall. Was this the spot where he had crawled through? Or was it somewhere else? He couldn't remember. He ran a dozen steps one way and then a dozen steps the other. Nothing.

Suddenly he heard a strange sound in the woods behind him. He swung around, but he saw nothing. Paladin looked into the forest. Now it no longer seemed friendly. It was dark and threatening, as if it were about to destroy him.

Desperately, Paladin searched the wall. He couldn't climb over; he couldn't break through. There was no way home.

"If you leave here, you will not find the way back." Shaddai's words rang in his mind.

The boy's eyes were wide with fear. He sat on the ground and hugged his knees to his chest and began to cry.

As Paladin huddled there, lonely and afraid, he remembered something else Shaddai had often said. "I love you so much." *Does he love me enough to come and find me?* wondered the boy. *Will he hear me if I call to him?*

"Shaddai, Shaddai! I'm so sorry I didn't listen to you! Please, come help me."

Paladin's plea had been heard by the one who loved him, even before it was spoken. For as the boy left Shaddai's workshop, the Maker had watched him as long as he could. When Paladin was out of sight, Shaddai turned, not to take up his work but to remove his apron. He hung his tools on the wall. Then he reached into the corner and took the staff, the one he'd carved after he finished the wall.

Even before Paladin had reached the wall, Shaddai had left the shop. Even before Paladin had asked for help, Shaddai was on the way to give it. Even before the hole in the wall had closed, Shaddai had opened another. His strong hands pulled away the rocks until he could see into the forest.

With his staff at his side, Shaddai crawled through the hole. He left the village he'd made and set out in search of his child.